T0065557

ANNA PUSTAI

Memories
— *with the* —
Meadows

The Meadow Family's Journey

WESTBOW
PRESS®
A DIVISION OF THOMAS NELSON
& ZONDERVAN

Scripture quotations taken from the Holy Bible, New Living Translation,
Copyright © 1996, 2004. Used by permission of Tyndale House
Publishers, Inc., Wheaton, Illinois 60189. All rights reserved.

This is a work of fiction. All of the characters, names, incidents,
organizations, and dialogue in this novel are either the products
of the author's imagination or are used fictitiously.

WestBow Press books may be ordered through booksellers or by contacting:

WestBow Press
A Division of Thomas Nelson & Zondervan
1663 Liberty Drive
Bloomington, IN 47403
www.westbowpress.com
1 (866) 928-1240

Because of the dynamic nature of the Internet, any web addresses or
links contained in this book may have changed since publication and
may no longer be valid. The views expressed in this work are solely those
of the author and do not necessarily reflect the views of the publisher,
and the publisher hereby disclaims any responsibility for them.

Any people depicted in stock imagery provided by Thinkstock are
models, and such images are being used for illustrative purposes only.
Certain stock imagery © Thinkstock.

ISBN: 978-1-5127-4962-5 (sc)
ISBN: 978-1-5127-4963-2 (e)

Library of Congress Control Number: 2016911572

Print information available on the last page.

WestBow Press rev. date: 08/23/2016

Contents

Thank You...

Jesus Christ–I would never be able to write without You!

My Parents–Thank you for being such wonderful parents! You are always encouraging my writing!!

My Friends–You are all such a blessing to me, and are always so encouraging! Thank you!

Haleigh–You are such a wonderful editor! Thank you so much for taking the time to edit my book.

Chapter One

Night Adventures

12-YEAR OLD GRACE CLIMBED OUT of bed, eager to find a cozier blanket in her bedroom. There was a chill in the air- a sign that summer was ending. As she laid the blanket on top of her bed, she paused. She smelled a faint hint of smoke, and stood with fear filling her body. Suddenly the smoke alarm's ear-piercing sound warned the family of a fire. She ran to her ten-year-old sister Melissa. "Melissa! Fire!"

Grace yanked the covers off of Melissa's bed. "It's an emergency!" Grace felt a sudden feeling of panic cover her whole body.

"I have to grab my game," Melissa said, still obviously asleep.

"A fire!" Grace was now shouting as she frantically fumbled to find her pink heart slippers.

"What!? Where?" Melissa grabbed her slippers and robe and Grace and Melissa were soon crawling out of their room.

They crawled down the steps and ran to their family meeting place in the front yard. "I didn't realize how hard it would be to crawl out the door!" Melissa yawned.

"Oh, look! Here come James and Joshua! Oh! There's Dad and Isabella! Praise the Lord that they are safe!" Grace said. She and Melissa waved from the front yard. Four-year-old James was crying as they approached the front yard.

"Grace, can you call 9-1-1? I have to help Mom with Leah. Melissa, watch the twins with Joshua. Thanks. Oh here is the phone!" Dad frantically said, tossing Grace his cell phone.

"Yes, Dad," the children answered sleepily. Grace's throat suddenly felt dry as she dialed 911. The dispatcher answered.

"Hello? Yes we have a fire. My name is Grace Meadow…363 Apple Blossom Street, Litzitown, PA…umm…yes, almost. My Dad and Mom are getting my sister out of her room…610-346-0633…Kendra and Jacob Meadow…Thank you…Okay, yes." Grace glanced up at Melissa, relived that the dispatcher would stay on the phone until the help arrived.

"Is the help coming?" Melissa asked anxiously.

"Yes, the man said that the firefighters would be here soon. Mom and Dad should also be out here quickly." Grace said soothingly as she rubbed James' shoulder. James still expressed lots of fear and was sitting in Grace's lap.

"We are all out! I have Leah, and Dad is here. Grace, did you call the fire department?" Mom asked, joining the children with Leah, out of breath.

"Yes ma'am. The dispatcher is actually still on the phone." Grace said. Joshua looked at the end of their street and noticed a red firetruck drawing closer. Grace quickly held the phone to her ear and told the dispatcher.

"They're here! I really hope the house is safe. I wonder what happened?" Joshua asked, bewildered as a red truck pulled into their driveway.

Once the firefighters climbed out of their truck, one officer came over to the Meadow family.

"Hello, my name is Christopher. This should only take a few minutes. Stay calm and don't go back into the house." Officer Christopher commanded.

"Yes, Officer Christopher. Thank you for coming to put our fire out!" Dad said.

"You're welcome...it's my job!" Officer Christopher smiled. He returned to his truck and grabbed some supplies, then joined the other officers inside.

Minutes that seemed like hours went by; the Meadow family tried to wait patiently and remain calm, relying on God for the safety of their home. James and Leah had fallen asleep, sitting on their siblings' laps. Surprisingly one-year-old Isabella stayed awake on Mom's lap. The Meadows had a miniature neighborhood that consisted of only eighteen houses. They lived in a house with pale blue shutters and on the side of the house there was a small and gorgeous garden that had produced many vegetables the past summer.

Soon, the firefighters came out of the house with good news.

"The house had a small fire; it looks like there was a candle that was left burning," Officer Christopher remarked.

"Oh! I must have forgotten to blow it out! I am so sorry, everyone." Mom's cheeks flushed a bright red as she realized she had caused the fire!

"Everyone makes mistakes," said a woman in uniform sweetly as she took off her mask. "You'll need to find a place to stay for tonight, but in the morning, everything should be fine. Oh, and by the way, my name is Rebecca!" Officer Rebecca said.

"Your mask was scawy! We was sleeping and then we heawd the beep." Leah, who had just woken up and had noticed Officer Rebecca's mask, was now happy to talk to the officers.

Mom looked at Dad concernedly. "I'm not sure who to call... maybe the Kalkers or the Johnsons? Let's ask the Lord for wisdom. Officer Rebecca and Officer Christopher, is there any way we could pray for you or anyone you know?" Dad remembered that the officers were standing next to him and thought they could show God's love to them by praying for them.

"Oh, thank you!" Said Officer Christopher. "I am a Christian, and was saved when I was twelve. You can pray for my three year old to know Jesus. Her name is Sadie. I have four other kids; can you pray for them to draw closer to God?"

Officer Rebecca said, "I, um...used to be a Christian but I turned away because I saw Christians getting sick just like other people and I just didn't get it! I have three kids. Can you pray for one of them? My littlest-her name is Savannah-needs healing from her cold! She's only six months old. Oh, and my Mom... She broke her arm."

"Thanks! We will be praying for you, then. Officer Rebecca, maybe someday I can write to you or we can talk on the phone about sickness and Christianity!" Mom said.

"That would be nice." Officer Rebecca smiled and nodded at Mom in the dark.

Joshua bowed his head and began to pray, "Dear God, please help Officer Christopher's three year old, Sadie..."

Joshua soon finished, and as Mom and Officer Rebecca exchanged e-mails and phone numbers, Grace caught sight of a man in pajamas hurrying down the road towards them. It was Mr. Johnson, the Meadow's neighbor!

"What happened?" He asked, concerned, as he looked at the group.

"Oh! We had a fire and we were just praying for shelter for the night. Did the commotion wake you up?"

"Yes, but that's nothing to worry about. Come over! The kids are asleep, but Sarah is awake."

Mom and Dad gathered up the sleeping twins and Isabella, and the family followed Mr. Johnson to his house three doors down.

Thank you God! Melissa silently prayed as they entered the Johnson's yard. *This is such an answer to prayer!*

"Goodbye, Meadow Family!" called the Officer's waving goodbye.

"Thank you! Goodbye!" Mom called as she walked into the Johnson's house.

That night, as Melissa and Grace climbed onto the sofa bed together, Grace was deep in thought. Even in the dark she could see the outline of Leah curled up in an old sleeping bag.

"Melissa, it is so nice of Mr. and Mrs. Johnson to let us sleep here. I am so thankful to have a sister like you!" Grace sleepily whispered, but all she heard in return was snoring from the other side of the bed.

Chapter Two

Cleaning Up and Witnessing

THE SUN WAS JUST RISING as James rose up out of bed. He wondered where he was he had been asleep for half of the fire situation. He looked around and noticed that Joshua was in the room with him. *Wait a minute…am I at someone else's house?* This wasn't their house, but it looked familiar.

"Joshua, wake up…where are we?" James ran over to the other side of the bed.

"Oh, good morning, James. We're at the Johnson's house. You fell asleep when the officers told us it wasn't safe to stay at our house last night. We all prayed and Mr. Johnson let us stay here."

As the Johnsons began to dress and cook breakfast, the early-rising Meadow family was also in action. Grace and Melissa explained why they were at the Johnson's house to Leah, and Mom helped with breakfast. Dad had called the office and let them know he would have to stay home today.

During a breakfast of scrambled eggs and toast, the Meadows thanked the Johnsons for their generosity.

"You have no idea what an answer to prayer you were to us! We had just prayed for God to give us a place to sleep when you walked to our house." Dad said.

"We are so happy to be here for you! God must've told me to check on your family. You have been joyful, even though this hard situation," Mr. Johnson stated.

"Thank you for saying that. That is one quality that Kendra and I have been working on," Dad said as he helped clear the empty plates.

After breakfast was eaten, the rooms were cleaned up, and all the kids were dressed, Mom took the children home. As they walked home, they began to feel anxious about the condition of their home.

When they went inside the house, it smelled only slightly of smoke.

"It doesn't look too bad. Just a few burn marks on the wall and cabinets," Joshua remarked as he surveyed the damage in the kitchen.

Before starting the clean-up job, the Meadow family stopped in their tracks to thank God for all He had done for them.

In a half hour the smoke stains were thoroughly washed off of the walls. "I'll grab some paint from the basement." Dad announced. Mom and big kids started pulling down curtains to wash while Melissa babysat the little ones.

After a few hours of work, the Meadows sat down to a simple lunch of chicken salad sandwiches. Suddenly, the phone loudly rang. Mom didn't recognize the voice when she answered.

"Hi...this is Rebecca from the fire department. How are you all making out today?" Mom grinned as she remembered the conversation from the night before.

"We were just cleaning up and thanking God for sending you so quickly!"

"Thanking God? For the fire?" Officer Rebecca sounded perplexed.

"Sometimes God uses these situations to teach us lessons. We learned we can trust Him with our home and safety last night," said Mom, sensing Officer Rebecca's confusion.

"I think you are all an amazing family and would love to spend more time with you."

"You and your family are welcome to come for dinner sometime," Mom excitedly offered.

"That would be nice! I'll e-mail you to figure out a date."

Mom hung up and told the children all about the conversation.

Later that evening, the children enthusiastically chatted about a playdate they had planned for the very next day with the Swedsberrys, a family that went to their church. As they dressed for bed, the children grew even more excited for the next day.

As Joshua pulled the covers up to his chin, he heard a sigh from across the room.

"James? Are you still awake?"

"Yes. What if we have another fire tonight? I'm scared" James admitted.

"Well, I think God will take care of us no matter what," Joshua said, yawning. "Do you want me to pray with you?"

"Yes, Joshua." Joshua went over to his little brother's bed and asked God to watch over them while they slept. As he closed the prayer, James gave him a big hug.

Chapter Three

Surprises

WHEN THE CHILDREN AWOKE, THEY were in for a disappointing surprise. The twins appeared to have a stomach virus.

"Oh, I really wanted to play with the Swedberrys, Mommy! But my tummy hurts." James lay back on his bed, which was covered with toys and coloring books.

"I know, honey. We will invite the Swedberrys over again. I am going to move Leah into your room to keep you company. She can use the inflatable mattress. I will check on you every few minutes, okay?" Mom gently tucked James in.

Half an hour later, Mom carried Isabella down the stairs.

"Hi Mom! We are having breakfast, and we were wondering what school books we'll need today," Grace said.

"Well, let's try for a full day of school...grammar, spelling and vocab books, math, English and your reading time for fifteen minutes." Mom answered.

Grace winked at Joshua and Melissa; the children shared a secret. They had decided to "birthday plan" for Mom after their school work was completed.

Grace ate the last bite of her rice cake and peanut butter and put her green plate on the counter. She hurried into the family room, hoping to start with the subject she struggled with the most: grammar!

Melissa worked hard at her math problems. She finished twenty two problems after working for an hour.

"Yay! I finished grammar and math, and now I've finished English! Hooray! Melissa, are you still on your first subject?" Joshua asked.

"Um...yeah." Melissa felt like crying as she looked into Joshua's excited eyes.

"Joshua, Melissa is trying her best," Mom said gently.

"I'm really sorry, Melissa! Can you forgive me?" Joshua asked.

"Yes, of course!" said Melissa, feeling better. She went back to finish math and then moved to vocabulary.

As the school day passed, Mom checked on Leah and James from time to time. After finishing a spelling test with Grace, she climbed the stairs with Joshua, and Melissa.

"Mom, I have a feeling this is not going to be good!" Joshua suppressed a laugh. They paused when they heard giggling.

They ran down the hall and found Leah drawing with a sharpie on the wall!

"Look Mommy! I found markers in your room and I let James have the black one. We are practicing letters on the walls!" Leah smiled with pleasure.

"Oh!" Mom gasped. "Um....Leah, you will have to go back to your room! This is not a good idea! Sharpie is permanent! I think I remember that a magic eraser will help this. Leah and James never EVER do this again." Mom yelled, but quickly regretted it as she stared at the *L, I, O, S, K,* and *J* on the walls with scribbles. *They are only four.* She thought.

"Okie dokie!" James said.

"Can I help you clean up?" Leah asked with a serious expression.

After the next hour of scrubbing the walls with a magic eraser, the permanent marker finally started to lighten up.

Later on, Mom called the twins. "You know what, Leah, and James? As much as I was upset with you, I really should've been calmer. I am trying to be more joyful in every situation, and I got very upset about the mess, forgetting what really is important. Can you both forgive me?" Mom asked her four-year-olds.

"Yes, Mommy!" The twins said in unison.

After the children had finished their schoolwork, Grace, Melissa and Joshua gathered their secret surprise notebook and pen to plan for Mom's birthday. They moved into the laundry room and closed the door.

"Oooh, this will be fun! I have an idea already! A bag!" Melissa excitedly said.

"Great idea! I actually noticed that Mom needs a new one; the old bag ripped the other day. I was thinking that maybe we could get her a mug with pictures on it, too." Joshua suggested.

Grace jotted the ideas down in her notebook. "Okay. So a mug, tote bag, and I had the idea of getting a blanket with all of our pictures on it. Maybe we can pray and ask God to tell us what Mom wants."

Chapter Four

The First Day of School

"I'M SO EXCITED FOR TODAY!" Grace shouted as she bounded down the steep stairs. The first official school day, August 22nd, had finally come. During the summer, Mom normally assigned them small amounts of school, but the first day of school was a special day-it had finally come!

"What will we do first today?" Melissa examined a list of items Mom had posted on the kitchen marker board.

"Well, today we will have a half school day, take some school pictures after dinner, and ...I have a surprise planned!" Mom looked at Melissa, Grace, Leah, James and Joshua, who were seated around the school table.

"What is the surprise, Mom?" curious James asked.

"Oh, you'll see soon enough!" Mom grinned at her excited four-year-old.

"I am really excited to start the new writing curriculum that you bought, Mom!" All the children seemed eager to start the school year, and that brought her joy.

"We will be starting a co-op this year. I know this is new for all of you, but it will be a wonderful change. I actually went to one when I was a child, and I enjoyed it! We are going to visit the co-op on October 11th, and if we don't care for it, we'll try another one. Dad and I talked and prayed about the co-op, and so far God is telling us 'yes'!" I have a chore list for each of you to do also, but I think we will try to talk that over in our upcoming family meeting." Mom announced.

"So back to the surprise! After school, we will take a walk on a path called "Crosskey Paths" and stop at park rea near the path to eat popsicles. We will also take some potty breaks, since they have a restroom there. How does that sound?" Mom asked.

"Yay! I can't wait!" Cheers were heard around the room. The children thought it was a great idea!

"Before we go, I need to take orders on popsicles; they are my homemade pineapple, and grape kinds. We are going to pick up lunch on the way at a new drive- thru sandwich place."

After schoolwork was completed, Mom made a list of what kind of sandwiches each child wanted. While the children put their shoes on, Mom had packed a backpack cooler with popsicles and lots of ice.

They were off to the drive- thru place, ready for a fun family outing!

"Hey, my name is Jill, what I can get for ya today?" Said a lady's voice through the drive-through speaker phone.

"Hello! Could I please have one tomato chicken pesto... ham n' cheese that will be two of those... turkey and cheese, and two chicken salad sandwiches please?" asked Mom, consulting her list of sandwiches.

"Okay. Will that be all for you?" The lady's loud voice rang through the speaker.

"Yes, thank you!" Mom answered as she heard a crashing noise. She glanced at the back seat of the car; thankfully one of the children had only dropped a book.

"You are surely welcome. See ya at the window."

Soon they were off to the walking path, eating their delicious lunch on the way. "We are here!" Mom exclaimed. The path was surrounded by trees, and flowers. The lilies were especially pretty. As they began, Grace walked with Leah and Melissa walked with Joshua and James.

"We should be at a small bridge in about five minutes before the rest stop where we will have popsicles and a bathroom break. We can turn around there, too. All right, here we go!" Mom buckled crying Isabella into the small stroller. "I'm hoping that Izzy takes a nap while we are walking."

"Mom, Izzy is such a cute nickname. Did you just make it up?" Grace, who was observant, smiled at Mom.

"Yes, I guess I did!" Mom laughed as she pushed the stroller near a patch of gorgeous pink flowers.

"Oooh, pink pwetty, I mean prrretty flowers," Leah said as she and Grace spotted them. Leah still had some speech impediments, but was slowly working on them.

"Yes they are!" Grace agreed.

"Are you all enjoying yourselves?" Mom asked after Isabella had fallen asleep.

"Oh, yes! And look! Here is the bridge!" James bounced up and down.

"Yes, this is the bridge. We are almost to the rest stop! Would you like to jog ahead a bit? I am going walk, not jog, because I would love for Isabella to take a longer nap. Melissa, you can join Grace's and Leah's group."

The two teams set off in a jog and kept jogging until they entered the rest area.

"Hey! Is that Dad? Look! He brought our bikes...Oh, we can bike back to the car!" Melissa ran to with Dad, along with Grace, Joshua, Leah and James close behind.

"Is that Aunt Kara and the kids too?" Grace ran over to see her cousins with joy.

"Well, what a surprise!" Aunt Kara said hugging Mom.

"Wow! I didn't expect this! I brought extra popsicles. Do the kids want them? Did you take another path that meets here?" Mom asked.

"Oh, thank you, the kids would love them! Yes there is a path the other way," Aunt Kara said. Soon Dad climbed into his car and the Meadow children bid Dad, Aunt Kara, and their cousins goodbye.

The rest stop break was fun, and the bike ride to the parking lot was enjoyable. Mom pulled the twins and Isabella in a carriage that that attached behind her bike. Joshua pedaled to keep up with Mom, and Grace and Melissa followed close behind.

As they reached the car, the children were exhausted- except for Isabella who had slept half the bike ride and finally woke up.

Later on, Dad decided to take the kids outside to play a game of baseball while Mom prepared dinner. The front yard was filled with laughter and happiness. This had been an amazing first day of school for the Meadow family.

Chapter Five

Saturday Adventures

"GOOD MORNING, BOYS! TIME TO wake up!" Dad said as he opened the door of Joshua and James' room.

"Hi Dad! What a lovely day!" Joshua pulled the covers down and saw the sun shining through his curtains.

"Hi Joshua! I love your cheerful attitude! I can tell that the Lord is working in you on that. You boys can have some quiet time, get dressed, and come down around seven thirty. Mom and I are making waffles this morning," Dad announced as he placed Joshua's brown Bible, his devotional, and James' picture Bible on each of their beds.

"What are we going to do today?" sleepy James rubbed his eyes.

"Well, you know that the Johnsons and Kalkers are coming over at four fifteen, but Mom and I are discussing what else we should do today." Dad left the room and headed downstairs.

"I wonder what else we will do today. Do you want to get dressed first while I do my devotional and read my Bible?" Joshua asked.

"Yes!" James skipped to the bathroom, happy that he had a brother who loved him.

While the boys were taking turns in their room doing quiet time and getting dressed, the older girls helped Leah get dressed in the littler girls' room. Leah found one of her old church dresses, and decided to go downstairs to surprise Isabella with the dress.

Where is Isabella? Leah thought. Leah decided to go downstairs to investigate.

"Mommy? Where is Isabella?" Leah asked, puzzled, when she finally found Mom talking to Dad.

"Oh, hi honey! Isabella is playing with some toys." Mom pointed to the Meadow's pack n' play, which had been passed down from Grace all the way to Isabella.

"Here you go, Izzy. This is for you. She is so a cutie," said Leah. Most of the time, no one wanted to correct Leah's four year old expressions because they were so cute!

"Leah, did you look at your picture Bible? I set out a special activity in the family room for you, too!"

"No Mommy, I didn't. Can I bwing it up to my room like Grace, Joshua, and Melissa dow?" Leah asked hopefully.

"Yes, you may. I'll come and get you in five minutes when the others are ready for breakfast." Mom answered.

"Okie dokie!" Leah meandered back up the stairs.

When five minutes were up, all the children came bounding downstairs.

"Breakfast time!" Dad called.

"Yay, waffles! I love yummy, yummy waffles!" James grinned.

"Good! Dad and I were talking, and we decided that we could all play games together, or play outside, even though there isn't much room in our backyard." Mom glanced out the window at their small backyard with its tire swing and a tree.

"We were thinking it has been a busy week and we should lay low before our company comes. What would you each like to do?" Mom asked as she looked around the table.

"Playing games would be fun!" Joshua said, and the rest of the family agreed.

"I have an idea! Why don't we each make a game? For the twins, they can pick a board game that we already own," Melissa suggested.

"I like it! Let's get to work after chores and breakfast!" Dad said, flipping a waffle.

After breakfast and chores, the family started getting ready to play and design games. *I think I'll make a game about memorizing God's word,* thought Melissa. She cut out easy memorization verses she had copied by hand. Then Melissa made a small prize of homemade chocolate bananas that she had put in the freezer just a few weeks ago.

"Are we all ready?" Dad looked around the room after a half an hour had gone by.

"Yes!" All the children chanted.

"Here are the two teams. One, two, one, two...."

It turned out that team one was Mom, Melissa, Leah, and Joshua, and team two was James, Grace and Dad. Team one went first. Joshua's game was about running races, and he read Bible verses about exercise. The winning team was team two, and they each received an exercise goal, which was a journal to keep for exercising each one's faith.

Soon it was time for Grace's game.

"For my game, you have to draw a simple picture of anything you'd like. I am going to base this game on a part of my favorite verse in Ephesians."

"Ephesians 2:10 says 'For we are God's masterpiece.' (NLT) So when you are done, I want each of you to stand up if you are going to memorize this verse, and write it down on your "masterpiece."

"I know this isn't really a competition game, but still, whoever memorizes it gets a memory verse card with the verse on the front of it!" Grace smiled as many drawings with Bible verses came her way, and the whole family stood up.

"That was really fun! You children put God's word, the most important book, into your games. I am really proud of you!" Mom hugged each of the children.

Chapter Six

Dinner Get-Together

THE DAY CONTINUED WITH CLEANING and cooking as the family prepared for the Johnsons and the Kalkers. Finally, the Johnson family was at the door!

"Hi, Kendra! It's been so long since I've seen you!" Mrs. Johnson hugged Mom.

"Hello Sarah! It is so nice to see you! How have you been?" Mom asked.

"Oh good! We have been busy. The kids are almost done with school, but it has been hard with trying to get Naomi and Peter down for a nap with Ella just starting flute. All in all, though, we have been great!" Mrs. Johnson stepped aside as Mrs. Kalker and Maliah stepped inside, followed by Mr. Kalker and the two other children.

"How are you, Kendra and Sarah? I've missed you both lately!" Mrs. Kalker asked the rest of the ladies.

"Great! How about you?" Mom closed the front door.

"Oh, good! I have some news for you both: Baby Kalker number four is coming in early April!" Mrs. Kalker announced as she placed Maliah on her lap.

"Congratulations, Tracey!" Mom and Mrs. Johnson congratulated Mrs. Kalker.

Meanwhile, Grace was playing outside with Addie Johnson, Ella Johnson and Melissa. They ran around and played games.

"What have you been playing lately on the guitar?" Grace asked Addie.

"Well, I've been playing and learning the A chord and 'Holy, Holy, Holy.' I love guitar!" Addie answered Grace.

"You know, at our next family meeting I'm going to mention instruments. I've always been interested in the clarinet!" Grace looked over at Melissa and Ella, who had been listening to them.

"Good idea, Grace! I've always wanted to play the flute." Melissa glanced at Ella.

"I play flute. If you played, maybe we could play duets," Ella suggested.

"Great idea!" Melissa smiled with abundant joy at her friend.

The three families were soon gathered around the table.

"Thank you for this food!" James prayed. Grace ate spoonfuls of Mom's wonderful chili as she thought about how the Kalker's weren't saved. *It never crossed my mind till now that we should be praying for them. I'll talk to Dad or Mom...whoever comes to our room tonight.* Grace smiled at Addie across the table as she took a handful of tortilla chips.

"This has been so nice. Thank you for having us over!" Mr. Kalker remarked to Dad and Mom.

"You are welcome!" Dad said with a smile.

"Yes, thank you so much! By the way, I was wondering if you have any nice churches that you used to love or love now. Our church hasn't been that great lately. There is a new pastor who isn't as good at explaining and teaching as our old pastor," Mr. Johnson explained.

"Oh yes! We love our church! Here, I'll give you the name of it. It only takes about ten minutes to get there."

Dad jotted a few words on the paper. It said:

Calvary Chapel Mallard Burrow

113 Calvary Chapel Mallard Burrow Downingtown, PA

It meets at: 9:30

Dad passed the note to Mr. Johnson. "Here you go, Joe."

"Thanks, Jacob! We will hopefully visit soon, as long as all of us are well." Mr. Johnson stuffed the note into his front pocket.

After the delicious dinner and clean up, the families talked for a while.

"Noah, Andrew, and Naomi," Leah led her friends to baby Isabella, "this is Izzy. I know you have seen her before, but she's really cute, and on her birthday in August, she turns two! Guess what? She calls Mommy 'Mama.' Mommy says that I said 'Mama' too when I was small!" Leah held Isabella's chubby hand and placed a kiss on her cheek.

"My Mommy is going to have a baby just like Isabella!" Andrew remarked, and he looked at Isabella.

"Time for dessert!" Mom called from the kitchen. Mrs. Kalker hugged Mom.

"I am so sorry, but we have to leave! Thank you for hosting this! We will have to host something. Maybe a week before Thanksgiving? By the way I keep forgetting to tell you my e-mail address. I have known you for two or three years now and I still am so forgetful. Mine is "Tracey K 1 3 3 at fast mail dotcom." All right, goodbye Kendra!" Mrs. Kalker ran to catch up with her family outside.

"Mom?" Mom heard a voice as she met Grace. "The Kalker's aren't saved. I meant to tell you at bedtime, or Dad, but it's just too important! Could I grab our family's homemade tracts? I could run out before they leave?" Grace motioned to the gospel tracts on the nearest front hall table.

"Yes. Then come right in for dessert." Mom smiled at her daughter. Grace enthusiastically reached for the door. She sprinted across the lawn, and called to the Kalker family.

"Wait! I wanted to give this to you!" Grace handed the tract to Mrs. Kalker.

"Tracey, you know I think religion stuff is useless," said Mr. Kalker as he glanced at the paper.

"Well, Levi, let's just take it home, and check it out." Mrs. Kalker thanked Grace and left for home. Grace felt an immediate pang of sorrow for Mr. Kalker and thought about it as she walked back to the house.

"Hi, honey! How did it go?" Mom was waiting at the screen door.

"Oh, Mr. Kalker thinks religion is…." Grace gulped. "Useless. Mrs. Kalker seemed interested, though."

"I'm sorry that happened, but I'm glad Mrs. Kalker was interested. We will have to start praying for the Kalkers. The rest of the family is in the kitchen eating dessert with the Johnsons, except the twins and Isabella. It's almost seven thirty, and that is their bath time. Dad is up with the littler ones. Mr. Johnson went home with Noah and Naomi, and baby Peter is sleeping on Mrs. Johnson's shoulder." Mom walked into the kitchen with Grace. Grace sat next to six- year- old Katie.

"Hi, Grace! Where were you?" Katie asked thoughtfully.

"I was trying to tell the Kalkers about Jesus by using a tract." Grace bit into a cookie.

"I love Jesus! Yesterday, I asked Jesus to come into my heart!" Katie smiled.

"I love him too! Congratulations! That is wonderful! Wait right here." Grace walked quietly up the stairs in case Dad was rocking Isabella to sleep. Then she grabbed a devotional for four- to- eight year olds. She already had a copy of it since that year, for her birthday, she had received a copy from her Aunt and Grandma.

When Grace handed the pink book to Katie, she squealed. "Thank you!" said Katie.

"You are welcome!" Grace said with pleasure.

As Grace said goodbye to the Johnsons, she noticed Mrs. Johnson's bag. Grace took a mental note to tell the others that they should get a cute personalized bag for Mom as a birthday gift.

After baths, showers, and bedtime prep, Grace and Melissa were about to go to bed when Grace announced something. "This was a really fun day, and I am so glad our family knows Jesus!"

Chapter Seven

Family Meeting

Two weeks passed, and the sun was just peeking through the clouds. The bright sun in her face made Grace wake up. *Good! It's only six thirty!* Today there was supposed to be a family meeting! Grace jumped out of bed, happy to be up early and grabbed her outfit for the day. She hurried out of the room, hoping that the alarm didn't wake Melissa.

In the girl's closet, she quickly and quietly got dressed. After preparing for the day, she clutched the devotional and Bible that she treasured and decided to go to the kitchen to read it. As she read along in her bible, a Bible verse stood out to her:

Psalm 100:1-3 (NLT)

Shout with joy to the Lord, all the earth!
Worship the Lord with gladness.
    Come before him, singing with joy.
Acknowledge that the Lord is God!
    He made us, and we are his.
    We are his people, the sheep of his pasture.

"Grace? Good morning! You are up early today!" Mom remarked. She placed Isabella next to Grace on the floor with a blanket and a few toys.

"Yes! I was so excited about the family meeting today that I decided to get up early!"

"I'm so glad you are doing your quiet time. I call it... well you'll see tonight!" Mom suppressed a small laugh.

"I had my quiet time this morning also, but then, while Dad was writing down some things we would like to talk about at tonight's meeting, Isabella woke up. Is Melissa up yet? The others are getting dressed." Mom pulled frozen mangoes out of the freezer for a heathy smoothie.

"No, she wasn't up." Grace kept reading her devotional until it was time for breakfast.

"Do we have school today? I never looked at the clock! It's only seven ten!" Melissa looked at the clock, surprised by how early it was. She had just come downstairs.

"I wanted to get you up early because yes, we do have to do schoolwork, and then I have a project for you." Mom served each of the children a mango spinach smoothie.

"What kind of project?" Joshua bit into his muffin.

"Well, before the family meeting tonight, I was wondering if the twins would like to help me make a salad to go with our meatball sandwiches."

"Yes, Mommy! I want to be your helper!" James remarked as Leah nodded with round eyes.

"As for you three," Mom said to the older kids, "can you each take turns watching Isabella? Then you can decorate, and set out everyone's Bibles in case we read some verses, and maybe even a blanket for all of us to sit around," Mom said.

"Good idea!" Grace uttered as she peered at the green smoothie.

"This smoothie is amazing!" Melissa remarked. Grace nodded happily.

"We might as well call this more fun than a meeting! It is so great to have family time!" Dad said as he put on his coat.

"Yay! I can't wait!" Leah smiled.

After Dad left, the children did their schoolwork, and lunch was cleaned up, they decided to start preparations for the fun event happening that night. "What goes in the salad?" James asked.

"Well, first you and James wash the lettuce. Leah, you can wash the tomatoes." Mom turned the crockpot on, and set out potato rolls.

In the den, the older girls were working together to make it decorative while Joshua watched Isabella.

"Can we set out the big white blanket?" Melissa suggested.

"Great idea! I'll go grab our Bibles, and when I come back, I'll switch with Joshua and let him decorate too." Grace rushed out of the den and raced into each of the bedrooms. When she finished grabbing the Bibles, she and Joshua switched places.

"Hi, cutie pie! Do you want to play ball?" Grace picked the baby up and held her on her lap.

"Ball, ball!" Isabella's eyes lit up with pleasure.

"All right, here you go!" Grace rolled the ball towards Isabella for a while. Isabella seemed pretty content until she started to cry.

"What's the matter, Izzy?" Grace picked up the baby, and was about to take her to Mom, when she felt something wet.

"Oh, no! Your diaper leaked! I'll go find Mom for you." Grace found Mom in the kitchen.

"I just finished the meal, so perfect timing! Are the others done too?" Mom scooped the baby from Grace's hip.

"I think they are just finishing up."

"Good. We have worked hard, and it's Isabella's nap time, so finish the job please, and then you each may find something quiet to do. I'll be down in a little while. Leah, James, do you need a nap today?"

"Yes, Mommy, I'm tired!" James announced, but Leah decided not to nap.

Once the preparations in the den were finished, Grace, and Melissa sat on the couch crocheting birthday presents for Mom. Joshua and Leah played the card game 'Uno'. "Oooh, a green three. I don't have it, so I'll pick a card." Joshua and Leah were just about finished their second round when Mom came downstairs, holding a monitor.

"The decorations look great! I can play one round of 'Uno' before I go clean the bathrooms and type up some things for tonight!" Mom looked up at Grace and Melissa, who had quickly hidden the presents.

"Yes! That sounds fun!" Melissa jumped up, followed by Grace.

The rest of the afternoon went by quickly, and soon, at five fifteen, Dad arrived home.

"Meatbaw sandwiches-my favorite!" Joshua bounded into the kitchen just as Mom was serving the food. The family enjoyed the dinner, and was soon sitting on the white, fuzzy blanket for the family meeting.

"Well, first of all, lately we have needed to get more efficient with our chores, so I made this." Mom held up a poster with small pockets full of cards.

"Each child has a pocket, and each day, you will have a bunch of cards to do," Mom said as she showed the children her idea. "Then, when you are finished with a chore, you move its card to the blue pocket.

After Mom finished with her chore poster explanation, Dad started to talk. "Mom and I decided to look into more co-ops. You all will be visiting one soon, so Mom typed up some information about each of the co-ops for you to see." Dad read the information about the co-ops to the children.

"That was what I was typing!" said Mom, as she picked up sleepy Isabella.

"Two more things; I was talking to Mrs. Johnson, and she said that Ella plays flute, Addie plays guitar and their Mom teaches them both instruments. It turns out that Mrs. Swedsberry used to teach clarinet; she also plays violin and flute, and as you all know, I play cello! I also know you two older ones have been praying for an opportunity to play an instrument, so we've decided to start a music group. The families are coming over in a few weeks. What instrument would you play?" She asked, glancing at Joshua, Melissa, and Grace.

"A clarinet!" Grace shouted with joy.

"I would love to play flute!" Melissa cheerfully said.

"I have always been interested in the violin!" Joshua jumped up and down happily.

"I'm still talking to your cousins to see if they want to join the group." Mom said, and then she motioned to Dad.

"I had the idea of starting something called the 'Bible Time Goal'. You each have to read the Bible for twenty minutes per day for at least twenty days. The twins will have to color some pictures about the Bible stories, and Melissa or Joshua will read to them. In the mornings, Grace will be also help watch Izzy. By December, you will each get together with Mom and I, and you will tell us if you met the goal! Mom and I will give a prize to whoever listens to, colors pictures about, or reads the bible for our goal. Mom and I will also be doing the goal; it's a great habit to have!" Dad gave each of the older children a bookmark with a Bible reading idea.

After the family talked for a while, Isabella fell asleep. "I'll take her up to her crib," Melissa offered.

"Thank you, Melissa! That would be very helpful, but I would feel a bit less uneasy if Grace accompanied you." Mom smiled at her daughter.

Grace and Melissa quietly laid Isabella down for the night, and rejoined the others. The family meeting closed with a short family Bible verse of the night.

Chapter Eight

Frustration

A FEW DAYS AFTER THE enjoyable family meeting, Grace decided to mail the letters on the front hall table as a surprise for Mom. Grace, the early riser of the family, also decided to go through her stack of chore cards, finish some school, and run a mile. Just as Grace was tying her sneakers, she heard a whisper.

"Grace, its only six o' clock! What are you doing up this early? And when did you wake up?" Grace looked up to see Mom in curlers and pajamas.

"Oh, hi Mom. I meant to get my chore cards done and surprise you by mailing these letters. Also, I plan to run a mile and do school. Dad mapped out how many times back and forth to the Kalker's house is one whole mile. I woke up at five thirty and did my quiet time." Grace looked at her Mom.

"Grace Lynn Moore! That is really early! Go ahead and get everything done." Mom walked upstairs to hear Isabella crying.

"Oh! This has been a horrible night, and now a horrible morning!" Mom sighed, now rushing up the stairs.

When Grace opened up the mailbox, she noticed a letter inside. *Mom must've missed this letter yesterday!* The letter had her name on it; it was a letter from her pen pal, Emily Grace! She ripped the letter open to find a pretty bracelet and a small letter. It said:

Hello Grace!
Guess what? I got a puppy, and I named her Amelia!
She's really cute! What's your favorite type of dog?
Mine is a Portuguese water dog-that's what Amelia
is. I am glad we're pen pals! I enclosed a bookmark
for you. I hope you like it! Have a nice week!
Love your friend,
Emily-Grace

Once Grace finished her chore cards, and math, she started her mile. She ran up and down the sidewalk with Mom's permission. Mom had said to take Melissa as a buddy, and so she did. Once she was on her last lap, she thought about Mom. *I guess she was up with Isabella a lot last night. Maybe it's just a bad day for her!* Grace finished up her mile, pleased to have finished it, and walked tiredly to the front door with Melissa. It was locked! Grace rang the doorbell and knocked loudly until Mom appeared with a scowl on her face. "Grace! I just laid Izzy down. Now she's sure to wake up!" Mom stormed to the kitchen and laid out a milk carton and eight cups.

"Today we are having a small breakfast. I really wanted to make chocolate chip muffins, but I had to make something quick. I made a breakfast trail mix. It includes dried bananas, cheerios, dried berries I bought at the store a few weeks ago, and mini peanut butter balls-peanut butter mixed with Chex cereal. They're really small, about the size of cheerios. Isabella woke up five times, so I only slept two hours last night. Isabella..."

"Waaaa!" Isabella screamed.

"I'm so sorry, Mom!" Grace felt horrible that she had waken the baby up.

The next hour progressed slowly. Breakfast was finished soon, and after Isabella woke up, Mom brought her downstairs. After breakfast, Grace decided to write back to Emily-Grace. She had only written nine words "Dear Emily-Grace, Thank you for the sweet letter"-when she heard a crash. "Leah Eliza Moore!" Mom was raging with anger at the spilled milk all over the kitchen table.

"I...I was trying to help..." Leah stammered. Mom's mood calmed down a bit, but she was still angry.

"Look what you did! Now, grab a towel, mop up the milk ..." Mom stopped and glanced at the mess. "...And never, ever do that again!"

"I won't, Mommy."

Once Grace finished her letter, she thought things had calmed down. Melissa had just finished a story she was writing for a story contest, and after Grace had helped her check for mistakes, she decided to place it in the mailbox.

Just as Grace was about to talk to Mom, the doorbell rang.

"Hey Kendra!" Aunt Lizzie stood at the door.

"Oh! Hi Lizzie! I didn't know you were dropping over."

"Yes, I was going to a dentist appointment, and my dentist is only one minute away from here, so I decided to stop over." Aunt Lizzie hugged Mom.

"How are you feeling?" Mom smiled at Aunt Lizzie, who was expecting a baby in late October.

"I had one problem this morning. I couldn't find any clothes that fit me! I had to go to the store to buy maternity clothes! I went to the store in jeans, my pajama shirt, and this big jacket. I'm feeling fine, though. I have some news!" Aunt Lizzie showed an exciting expression.

Mom called the kids into the front hallway.

"Baby Meadow is going to be a girl!" said Aunt Lizzie. The children jumped around and hugged Aunt Lizzie.

"That's awesome news!" Melissa exclaimed.

Later that day, after Aunt Lizzie had left, Mom was still in her grouchy mood. Dinner was approaching, and that left Mom standing in the kitchen looking for something to cook. Just then, the phone rang.

"Hello...Yes, that's fine...I've had a horrible day...Well, Liz dropped over...she's going to have a girl...Well ...Oh...Yes...Love you...Goodbye."

As Mom had hung up the phone, Joshua bounded into the kitchen. "Who called?"

"Dad. We are going to have pizza tonight. Can you call your sisters and your little brother in here?" Mom asked.

"Yes, Mom!" He wore a grin on his face...Mom was smiling!

"I'm sorry for how I acted earlier. I was a bad example! I had a rough night's sleep. Then my alarm went off at four this morning and James sleep-walked into my room at four-thirty. Can you forgive me?" The children nodded, overjoyed to see their Mom in a better mood!

Chapter Nine

Mom's Birthday

It was Mom's birthday, and Dad and the children were surprising her. It was very early, and they had planned to make a scavenger hunt along with breakfast for Mom. Joshua leapt from his position near the oven. He wanted to put the twins' present for Mom on her nightstand before he, Melissa, and Grace brought her a slice of her favorite breakfast casserole.

After asking Dad for permission, the children woke up Leah and James.

"I have a present for Mommy, but it's a secret! Don't tell anyone. It's a pretty glittery box that Daddy helped me buy at the craft store! Mommy can write her prayer requests on paper and put them in it if she would like to." Leah held a serious expression on her face while talking to Melissa, and Melissa tried to hold the same expression, but couldn't help but smile.

"Wow! Mommy will love that! Can I help you get dressed in this pretty pink dress? Daddy is helping Joshua arrange all of our gifts for Mom in a pile, so when we deliver breakfast to her, she can open them!"

Leah nodded. "You can help me get dressed, but does Daddy have the special box? I wrapped it all by myself!"

"Yes, he does, but now it's time to get dressed!" Melissa was trying to stay patient with Leah.

"I like this dress." Leah pointed to the hand-me-down basket for Isabella.

"Leah, you have to wear this dress! You picked this out last night. Maybe tonight you can pick a different outfit for tomorrow. You wore that one when you were two, so I don't think it will fit you anymore, all right?" Leah nodded. Melissa felt happy that she resisted the temptation to yell at Leah.

Once Mom had eaten her breakfast, James said, "Mommy can you open the…" He covered his mouth. "I'm not supposed to tell!"

Mom nodded. "Yes, I will!" She looked at her nightstand. On it was one present and a balloon. As Mom ripped the wrapping paper, there laid Leah's gift for Mom; a small box, and James' gift; a small candle. "I bought that for you! It was only five dollars, and Grace helped me pay for it!" James announced.

"James, you weren't supposed to say that!" Grace gave James a playful smile.

"Thank you Leah and James!" As Mom looked in the box, she noticed a small piece of paper. It read:

> *Look where you might cook fried eggs,*
> *and you will find your next gift!*

Mom pulled the covers off the big bed, walked downstairs to the frying pan. There she found a gifts from Grace and Melissa. Grace had made Mom a beautiful crocheted purse, and a pack of pretty hair clips. "I sewed the flowers on the clips myself when you put Izzy down for a nap each day!" Grace hugged Mom, and Mom thanked Grace and then Melissa. Melissa had given Mom a pretty poem with her gorgeous word art in a picture frame.

Soon the family was off to find the last gifts. Joshua had given Mom a video that he had made with pictures of the year. "Dad gave me some help, but I did it mostly by myself!" Dad's gift for Mom was the best of all! He had given Mom a new milkshake maker and five books that Mom had on a wish list.

"How did you know that I wanted this? Did the kids tell you?" Mom asked.

"No, the kids didn't tell me, but I think the Lord put the idea into my head!"

After talking for a while, the children presented the personalized bag to Mom. She thanked the children and gave them a hug.

Once the rest of the family had eaten breakfast, Dad asked Mom what she would like to do today. "Well..." Mom thought for a moment. "What about go on a picnic or to a local garden? It's up to you all!" Mom said. Everyone agreed that a local garden would be fun to see!

Soon the family was ready, and off to the local garden. Dad pulled into a fairly empty parking lot with only six cars in it. "Wow. I wonder why it is so empty here? This parking lot is normally jammed packed!" Dad clicked his seatbelt off.

"Yes, I know! Well, it does appear to be kind of gray, maybe others thought it wouldn't be the best type of day to go to this garden. It is so gigantic that I don't think we'll make it through the whole garden in a couple of hours!" Mom unbuckled content Isabella; she was smiling from ear to ear.

"I agree that it's too big to make it through in a few hours. Do you want to pick a part of the garden you'd like to see? It seems to be sectioned off into four parts." Dad gazed at a folded map in his hand.

"I'd love for the kids to pick. Where would you like to go?"

"Why don't we go to the area with the one treehouse and pond? Look there is a hill too!" Joshua pointed to a section on Dad's map that read "Tiger Lily Pond Area."

"Yes, that would be fun!" The girls and James agreed with Joshua that it would be fun to explore and play in that area.

The family strolled through the entrance and a friendly woman met them there. "Hello, my name is Adora. Welcome to 'Anika's Garden!' Please enjoy your time here, and take your time to explore the different sections of our garden! We have a new section that was just added a couple of months ago. It's our fourth section, called the "Rest and Relaxation." There you could read a book under any of the lush trees and there are some gorgeous flowers around it, along with a walking path right through the beautiful scenery. Enjoy!" With that, Adora left to go inside a small café. *I never noticed a café when we came here a year ago. That must be new also,* Grace thought.

The Meadow family enjoyed walking along together, and soon got to the "Tiger Lily Pond Area." The twins ran up and down the hill several times with Joshua, Melissa and Grace, as Mom and Dad sat on a small bench with Isabella to watch. "It is truly wonderful here..."Mom paused as she felt a water droplet on her arm. "It actually feels like it's starting to rain!" Just then it started to pour.

"Let's run back to that café and we can eat lunch there," Dad suggested, and everyone quickly agreed.

After a quick run with Isabella, James and Leah in the stroller, they arrived at the small café. Soon the family was seated, enjoying their lunch. "It doesn't look like we will be able to go back out to the garden again. I'm really sorry. Maybe another day we can come back here," Dad said as he looked at the Doppler on his weather app.

"I feel like we ruined Mom's birthday." Joshua looked upset.

"No, nothing ruined my birthday!" Mom said enthusiastically.

"What!?" Melissa looked surprised.

"Eating together in a café, and doing anything with my family is the best thing I could ask for!" Mom smiled. "This has been a perfectly memorable birthday!"

Chapter Ten

Being a Blessing

ONE MORNING IN EARLY OCTOBER, Mom opened her eyes to a gray sky pouring with rain. "Ouch!" She exclaimed.

"What's the matter?" Grace asked as she walked into the room. Dad had left for a business trip to Maryland early that morning.

"I have a horrible headache. Do you children think you could make breakfast today? It's just toast and fruit. Grace felt confident that she could, but tried not to feel nervous about waking up Isabella and taking care of her the whole day.

"Yes, Mom, I'm sure I could. Should I wake Isabella up now?"

"No, wait till seven forty five at least. You can have a day off of school even though it's a weekday. I should be down by eight at the latest. You can feed Izzy tiny cubed pears that I put in the fridge, and tiny bite size pieces of toast." Mom felt her head and groaned. "Uh, and Grace."

"Yes, Mom?" Grace seemed even more concerned.

"Please grab me the phone and thermometer. I'm going to see if Aunt Kara, Grandma, or Mrs. Swedsberry can come over, I think that it might be a long day for me. Mrs. Swedsberry said if I ever needed any help, she would be fine to lend me a hand.

I think I might be running a fever, and I might have a cold flu." Mom sighed.

"Okay." Grace grabbed the items Mom had asked for. Mom took her temperature and sighed.

"I do have a fever: one hundred and one." Mom dialed the phone just as Grace was leaving the room.

"Hi Kara...this is Kendra...oh...yes, I have a fever and a horrible headache! Yes...that would be wonderful...Okay... thanks again...see you soon." Grace walked into Mom's room with Melissa, Joshua and the twins.

"Aunt Kendra and the kids are coming over in about a half hour. She said she is bringing donuts!" Mom closed her eyes and took a sip of mint tea that Grace had brought upstairs for her.

Half an hour later, Grace heard a knock at the door. "I'm here!" Aunt Kara put her arms around Grace and said, "You are getting to be very responsible, bringing tea to your Mom and finding all the things that she needed! It's so nice to see you!" After hugging Grace, Aunt Kara pulled out her hair tie. Her long straight dark brown hair was down to her hips just like her daughter, Faith.

"Grace!" Faith, who was eleven ran over to Grace and hugged her. She soon was hugging Melissa, and then Leah. The girls hugged and then ran into the kitchen to prepare a spot for the donuts.

"I'm sorry Aunt Kendra's sick. You must've been scared!" Faith smiled graciously at her cousin as she gave her a napkin. Grace was so happy to have her cousins over! What a start to the day it had been!

The children passed the next hour by eating breakfast and cleaning the house.

"This is a way to bless Mom. The Bible says to do things as if doing them for the Lord. I want to do that, so I am going to surprise Mom by emptying the dishwasher, since it's not one of my chore cards!" Joshua willingly opened up the dishwasher, and steam blew into his face.

"That's a goodie goodie idea! Let's give Mommy a surprise!" James hurried over to the cabinet and put on rubber gloves.

"What can *I* do?" Leah asked.

"Well, Leah, you can help by cleaning the baseboards and watering your Mom's garden. I noticed it when I pulled into your driveway. It's very well cared for. Your Mom would be very happy if you did that! Let's all clean the house and be a blessing!" Then Aunt Kara pointed to the windows.

"Faith and Julia, can you clean the windows? Then Timothy, you and Melissa can take the garbage to the curb and get the mail. That leaves Matthew to wipe the table down, and Grace can help me organize the laundry room." The children and Aunt Kara got to work tidying the house and working outside.

Melissa hurried outside with her cousin Timothy.

"Melissa?"

"Yes, Timothy?" Melissa turned her glance to Timothy.

"I said something mean to Julia, and I don't think she will ever forgive me!" Timothy's words exploded out of his mouth.

"What did you say? Did ask her forgiveness?" Melissa felt excited that he asked her about this problem, but sad that it seemed like he hadn't told anyone else.

"Uh..." Timothy paused. "I told her she wasn't a nice sister, and...and that I didn't want to play with her anymore...but I didn't ask for forgiveness. Maybe I should. Thanks Millie!" Timothy rushed back to the house.

Well, so much for him helping with the chores, but I guess I was a blessing to him and that is what matters. Millie, what a cute nickname for me! Melissa thought as she looked into the pile of mail. No letters for her...only one for Joshua from Liam, his pen pal from Northern New Jersey. Melissa looked closer at the pile and gasped. There sat a letter from the story contest readers. She quickly opened it up and jumped for joy. It read:

Dear Melissa,

We read your story called "Loving the Lord," and we are happy to say that you are the winner! Not only will you receive a bound copy of your book, but you will get a big basket of writing tools such as pens, notebooks, etc.! Congratulations! You should receive your manuscript and the basket in the mail soon! E-mail me if you have any questions at indigopublisher@fallfree.com

Sincerely,

Indigo Meppepa

Melissa ran into the house and told her cousins, aunt, and siblings the news. They were all so happy for her.

"I was just about to check on Kendra-your Mom. I'll tell her the good news, Melissa! Let's all get back to our chores and duties, though. Never stop being a blessing!" Aunt Kara hurried upstairs, and all the children went back to their jobs.

"Joshua, you got a letter in the mail from Liam, your pen pal. Here, I'll put it on the table for you!" Melissa remarked as she hurried to take out the garbage. *I think that the Holy Spirit told Joshua to be a blessing today for Mom!* Melissa skipped happily down to the driveway.

Chapter Eleven

Planning Day

OCTOBER 15ᵀᴴ HAD ARRIVED- THE planning day for Mom's music group! Melissa opened up her blinds and sighed. Another rainy day! The rain poured down from the sky like buckets. She glanced over at Grace's bed, which was made. *She has probably been up for a while and didn't want to wake me up.* Melissa looked at the clock. It was 6:28. Melissa opened her eyes wider than before, not believing she had really waken up early! As Melissa walked to the closet to lay out her clothes, she tripped and stubbed her toe. "Ouch!" She exclaimed. Sometimes she wished that their room wasn't always crowded. It wasn't that their room was cluttered, but the two beds didn't fit very nicely. It was almost like a maze! As she opened up her Bible to 1ˢᵗ Thessalonians 5: 16-18 (NLT), she read a verse: "Always be joyful..." Melissa stopped as she thought about all the complaining she had been doing that morning. Melissa prayed, "Dear God, I am sorry that I've been complaining. Please forgive my sins. Amen."

"Melissa, Mom sent me to tell you that breakfast is in ten minites." Melissa jumped as she saw James in the doorway.

"Oh, okay!" Melissa thanked James, surprised he was up also, and quickly dressed herself in jeans and a ruffled pink, short-sleeved shirt. Today was the meeting for the music group, and Melissa didn't want to look sloppy… not that she ever did!

"Well…yes I do understand." Mom and Dad were talking in the living room while the children were preparing for the day, and Grace writing in her diary on the front porch.

"Yes, dear. Should we tell the children soon?" Mom saw Joshua coming nearer and motioned to Dad. "Yes, let's do it tonight. Why, Joshua? What's the matter?" Dad asked.

"Well, uh, I had a question. Wh-why.." Joshua began, but was interupted by a clatter and cry.

"Help!" It was Leah's voice. The three of them rushed to find Leah at the bottom of the stairs.

"Leah? Oh no!" Grace appeard worried as she opened the front door. "I was writing on the porch when I heard a cry."

"Can you go like this? Whoo—Ahh." Grace breathed in and out.

Leah's face turned red for a moment, but then she said, "N… no! I coul-couldn't! Y..yow!" Leah pointed to her arm. "It feels hard hurt!"

"You mean hurt hard?" Mom pulled Leah onto her lap just as they heard a roll of thunder. A face appeared at the top of the stairs; it was Melissa.

"What happened?" Melissa had concern witten all over her face.

"I fell down the stairs! Mommy! I heard funder!" Leah cried.

"Now, its all right. Can you move it like so?" Mom moved her arm slightly.

"Yes, I can. I feel better!" Leah responded to Mom.

"It seems like you slipped and knocked the wind out of yourself." Mom carried Leah to the kitchen and placed the startled four year old in her seat.

Soon Melissa appeared with James holding her hand and Isabella in her arms. The baby looked intent and smiled. "Ma-ma!" Isabella reached out her arms to Mom.

"Thank you Melissa! I didn't hear her. It must've been when Leah fell down the stairs."

"What?" James wondered with curiosity.

"I'll tell the story!" Joshua told James the tale of Leah's fall.

After breakfast, the three Meadow girls decided to tidy up the family room. Just as they were about to talk to Mom, Joshua appeared.

"I accidentally heard Mom and Dad talking about a house. I didn't mean to eavesdrop…"

"Oh Joshua!" Melissa worried out loud. "I sure hope nothing is the matter! Maybe the house is too much money and they can't pay for it and maybe…"

"Melissa, be careful what you say," Grace whispered. "Leah might be paying attention to the conversation."

"Oh, sorry!" Melissa mouthed.

"And besides, if any of that did happen, which I doubt it will, God will take care of us," Joshua earnestly said, and the girls nodded intently.

Soon the Johnsons were at the door, followed by Aunt Kara and the cousins, Faith, Timothy, Julia and Matthew. Then, in came Mrs. Swedsberry.

"Kristen! It's been a while since I've seen you!" Mom flew from her seat and hugged her friend. Mom had known Kristen Swedsberry since she was only in 6th grade.

"Oh hi Kendra! I have a book that you lent me a year ago. Here it is! I am so sorry it took me this long to give it back to you!" She placed her two-year-old son, Benjamin on the carpet of the living room.

The meeting ran smoothly for Mom, and the children were having a blast in the family den playing games with their friends. Soon Mom called all of the children into the living room. "We are going to start a group on Tuesdays at one o' clock each month. You will each practice your instrument and report to your teacher at the end of the week." Mom grinned from ear to ear.

"So, I will teach flute and guitar, Mrs. Hallmer (the Meadows children's aunt) will teach oboe, Mrs. Swedsberry will teach violin and clarinet, and Mrs. Meadow will teach cello." Mrs. Johnson told the children.

The children were excitedly chatting to one another yet again. Then Mom told the kids that the four- year -olds were going to start also! This was too much for the little ones! They started to giggle, jump, and enthusiastically smile at one another.

Later that day, Mom said, "We'll start in January!" The children were wondering why they had to start after such a long time, but Mom didn't explain to them.

At four o'clock in the afternoon, after saying "hello" to the children and Mom, Dad said, "We have some news for you, children." Dad cleared his throat. "And we want to take you to a special place to say it." The children were cheerful; the last time Mom and Dad had big news, it was that baby Isabella was coming.

Dad drove them to a house near a lake and parked the car. The sign next to the house read "OPEN HOUSE!"

Chapter Twelve

Surprises

"Mom, Dad? W..why are we looking at an open house?" Grace's voice trembled as she saw another family approach the house.

"Honey," Mom hugged Grace as she frowned. "God has been calling Dad and I to buy a new house. We want to have privacy in our backyard when you children go outside to play, and it seems like you are all tripping over one another in your rooms."

"WOW! God is giving us a new house? Is this the house we are going to buy?" Joshua smiled, looking around the pretty house as they approached the front doorway.

"Well, we are just visiting the house, not buying it at the moment." Dad noticed a friendly faced lady; the thought occurred to him that she must be the realtor.

"This is all so..so sudden! Why did you decide this so soon? I am so upset that we are moving. I love our house!" Melissa was holding back tears, which made Leah start to wail.

"Well, I think everyone has mixed emotions about this! Why don't we look around the house before getting upset about everything?" Mom suggested as the kids began to calm down.

"Okay," five voices said in unison.

As the Meadows walked to the front door, the realtor, who was standing there, smiled at them.

"I'm Fiona Lerrs. Are you here to visit this house?"

"Yes. It's so nice to meet you!" Mom picked up Isabella, who was crawling on the carpeted floor.

"Let me show you around. I am so sorry for the musty smell. There is actually a small oil leak, nothing to worry about!"

Dad and Mom exchanged looks as if they had been hit with bad news. Grace, Melissa and Joshua, who knew what an oil leak was, had a sudden wave of unsteadiness sweep through their bodies.

As the Meadow family gazed into a huge kitchen with marble countertops, they were without words. This kitchen was enormous! "How do you like this house?" Ms. Lerrs gestured to the house. After looking at this house, Mom and Dad thought it was oversized.

"Well, it might be a bit big for our liking. Maybe we will keep looking," Dad said and Grace breathed a sigh of relief. This house was horrible! And the musty smell made it even worse.

On the way home, the family discussed the house. "Maybe next time we will stick to looking at a rancher!" Melissa suggested, and everyone started to laugh.

"I liked the hugenourmeous part of it! Maybe sometimes I would get lost, but then I could play that I was lost in a jungle!" James and Joshua appeared to be excited about the prospects of buying a new house.

"You mean enormous? It's still pretty early... about six o'clock... and I think we are going to eat grilled cheese tonight." Mom announced.

"I don't like grilled cheese!" Leah uttered from the backseat of the car.

"I'm sorry, Leah, but since it was a pretty busy day, I didn't have time to make a huge, scrumptious meal." Mom, who sat in the passenger seat of the car, smiled at the gorgeous leaves that were scattered through a half-bare tree.

"Okay, I'll try to be happier about eating grilled cheese. But…" Leah paused and scrunched her face up. "I'll have to eat it holding my nose!"

"Look! The trees are red in this pasture, and there are horses, too. How beautiful!" Melissa admired the autumn trees lining the road. They appeared to mark entrance to a horse pasture.

"Yeah, the trees are really pretty!" Grace agreed.

The family enjoyed viewing the trees, but soon they turned into their wet driveway. As Leah hopped out of the car with James, they both splashed in the puddles.

"Whee!" Giggles were heard as Dad approached the two four year olds.

"Time to go in you two. It's getting dark, and I'm sure you don't want to be out here while the rest of us are eating dinner!"

"No, but I want to stay out here and splash with Leah." James obviously didn't want to go into the house.

"Be joyful in everything we do, even if it's something that you don't want to do, okay?" Dad took James' hand, and Leah followed them inside. As the twins and Dad opened the door, they were surprised by a sound from the driveway behind them.

"Well, hello!" Aunt Lizzie and Uncle Mason walked through the door.

"Lizbeth and Mason? What a surprise!" Dad smiled at the guests approaching.

"Oh! I forgot that we invited them over for tonight!" Mom had red flushed cheeks and looked embarrassed. Dad reassured her that making grilled cheese would be fine.

The guests hung their items on the coat hooks. "I'm sorry I didn't warn you, but I actually brought a full meal. I hope you haven't started anything yet!" Aunt Lizzie held up a salad and Uncle Mason held a crockpot full of chicken.

"Well, thank you so much! No, I had forgotten you were coming over, and after a long, long, day I was hoping to make a simple meal of grilled cheese."

Later on, after dinner was served, the family had made their way into the den. "I think it's time for us to leave," Aunt Lizzie yawned.

"Keep us posted on baby Meadow!" Mom hugged her sister-in-law.

"Yes, I'm sure she will be born soon. Her due date was yesterday!" Aunt Lizzie remarked.

Just as Mom was just crawling into bed that night, her phone buzzed loudly. She was about to turn it off when something caught her eye. It read, "Call from Mason Meadow." Mom gasped. She quickly called Uncle Mason in the hallway, hoping not to wake up Dad or the kids, and found out that Aunt Lizzie was in the hospital with Uncle Mason. He said that the doctors thought the baby would be born soon! Mom, tired from the long day, fell asleep in the hallway after she had finished the conversation with Uncle Mason. She was too tired to walk back to the master bedroom.

Chapter Thirteen

Dinner with Officer Rebecca

THE NEXT DAY, THE MEADOW family found out that Aunt Lizzie had given birth to baby Eleanor-Rose early that morning. The family decided to buy a gift for the new family member and visit them.

The Meadows drove to the store and bought baby Eleanor-Rose an outfit and Aunt Lizzie and Uncle Mason a special card and ornament with a picture-holder that said "Family" on it. They were off to the hospital.

"Who are you visiting?" A secretary whose name read "Delany"sat at a desk.

"Lizbeth and Mason Meadow." Mom picked up Isabella, who was starting to let go of the furniture and try to walk.

"Lif Lif!" Isabella pronounced and then smiled.

"Are you trying to say Liz, Liz?" Melissa grinned at cute Isabella.

"All right, room two hundred one." The lady glanced up at Isabella and said, "What an adorable baby you have! What is her name?"

"Isabella." Grace held out her arms to her baby sister, and Isabella immediately crawled to Grace.

Grace tapped quietly onto the door of room two hundred one. Uncle Mason answered. "Hello! Ellie-Rose is awake, but crying."

"Aww! She's so sweet!" Mom smiled at her sister-in-law, who was beaming with joy.

"Thank you. She is a gift from the Lord. We are calling her Ellie-Rose, but her full name is Eleanor-Rose Meadow."

Grace, Melissa and Joshua took turns holding Ellie-Rose with Mom and Dad. The baby had dark brown hair and dark blue eyes, and she wore a soft hat that had a pretend leaf crocheted into it. "How adorable!" Melissa whispered as she held the sweet baby and smiled at the sight of a tuft of hair that was sticking up from under the baby's hat.

"I'm sorry to say it, but we have to go." Dad picked up Isabella who was again trying to toddle along. Mom nodded.

"I agree. The children have school to work on, and then we are going to be cleaning later." Mom hugged her sister-in-law and congratulated the new family once more before the Meadow family waved goodbye.

"A...B...C...D..." The alphabet song was being performed in the living room by Leah while Melissa worked on math, Grace worked on grammar, and Joshua was helped Mom in the bedrooms upstairs, since he had finished school.

"Grafe! Grafe! Up!" Isabella clapped her chubby hands before smiling.

"You are a cutie pie!" Grace left her grammar workbook on the table and picked Isabella up, placing her on her lap.

"Melissa!!" Leah's voice was interrupted by a scream.

"What?" Melissa frantically ran to the living room after exchanging a worried look with Grace. Grace and Isabella followed Melissa, who was now running.

"James and I wanted to make cupcakes as a supwise for Mommy, but then James burnt his hand when he tried to get my mix out of the oven." Leah seemed extremely worried for her brother who had tears rolling down his face.

"Where did he burn himself? And did you ask someone before putting something in the oven?" Grace questioned.

"Um...my whole...arm! And...no, I didn't. " James wailed. Mom and Joshua sprinted into the kitchen.

"I'll take care of this; don't worry." Mom reassured Grace and Melissa.

Brrring.....brring.....brring! The phone rang, and Joshua answered, "Hello? This is Joshua Meadow... Oh yes...yes...my Mom will be right there!" Joshua ran into the den, where Mom was talking to the girls and Isabella and James were playing with a train set. "Mom, Officer Rebecca is on the phone. Do you remember her?" Mom nodded, and took the phone, thanking Joshua.

"Oh hi... this is Kendra...yes, yes... oh, tonight could work for us...or maybe next week even...well, no worries...yes, of course... goodbye!" Mom beamed with joy. "Officer Rebecca and her three kids are coming over for dinner!"

"Oh! How wonderful! What are her kid's ages and names?" Joshua asked.

"Jane is three, George is two, and Savannah is seven months old. She told me that her husband died of cancer three months ago. I was sad to hear that. These kids are probably feeling sadness along with Officer Rebecca. She told me to call her just Rebecca and for you to call her Mrs. Liether, but I keep forgetting. We have to be Jesus to the Liethers!" Mom explained to the children and they nodded seriously.

"That *is* sad!" Grace agreed with Mom. After talking with the children, Mom quickly called Dad to tell him that Mrs. Liether was coming over.

Later that day, after Mom was prepared for dinner and Dad came home, the Meadows heard a knock at the door. "Rebecca! How nice to see you again!" Mom smiled at the two children and Mrs. Liether, who was holding a baby.

"It is nice to see you! It's also nice to be here without putting out a fire." Mrs. Leither laughed along with Mom and Dad.

"My name if Jane." A little girl told Leah, who was in the hallway next to Dad.

"Oh, hello! I am Leah! Awe you four?"

"No, but soon I will be! In Novembah!" Jane quickly skipped away, looking for her Mom, but Mrs. Leither was no longer standing by the door.

"Wh...where did Mommy go?" Jane looked worried until Melissa quickly led her to Mrs. Leither.

"Time for dinner!" Dad called as Grace looked around the kitchen. There was a big pot of tomato soup, a huge salad with lots of condiments, and a platter of chicken salad sandwiches.

"Yum! This looks good!" Grace commented as everyone took their places at the dining room table.

"Let's pray. Do I have any volunteers?" Dad asked, and after Mom quickly accepted, she prayed.

"Thank you for having us over! I actually have a question." Mrs. Leither glanced at Mom, whose hazel-colored hair was pulled back into a ponytail.

"Yes, what is your question? I'd be happy to answer it!" Mom excitedly smiled at Mrs. Leither.

"Well, my husband was a Christian, but like I mentioned on the phone, he became sick and died. I never understood why. I know I asked this a month or so ago, but I just don't understand." Mrs. Leither fed her baby mashed sweet potatoes and focused on Mom.

"Well, you know, it's funny, I saw a verse today while I was reading my Bible and it really spoke to me! It was about how God makes everything happen for a reason. Here is an example: what if I fell and broke my arm, I had to go to the emergency room, and they found out I was extremely sick? Maybe while I was in the hospital, God would teach me lessons I would never have learned in another situation! These type of situations happed to each and every one of us. I am learning right now to be joyful in all circumstances."

"Wow! I never thought of it that way! That makes me feel so much better!" Mrs. Leither, Mom and Dad talked for a bit more after that.

That makes me so happy to think that Mrs. Leither understands Mom and Dad and wants to know Christianity! Joshua smiled at the thought.

Chapter Fourteen

House- Hunting

ONE WEEK HAD PASSED, AND the Meadow family was busy with house-hunting and school work. They were on their way to visit a house in Hickory Valley, only fifteen minutes away.

"Hmm..." Joshua studied his book and put it down, obviously frustrated. "Mom, I can't figure out this mystery and I am getting extremely frustrated with it! It's making me hot."

"Well, honey, why don't you do something else to get your mind off of it for a little while?" Mom soothingly spoke to her son in a soothing tone. It was an early Saturday morning, and there was a chill in the air outside. They had decided to make today their "house-hunting" day.

"Here! Here it is. Oh, it's beautiful! Look at all the land." Mom was obviously excited at the sight of the house.

"Yes, it does look like a lot of land. Today we're going to look at this house, one nearer to our house, and then one about a half hour away. Let's all hop out!" Dad parked the car and helped unbuckle James and Leah. "I think we're all set. Stay together, and remember: no wandering or running in this house."

"Okay!"

As they entered the house, Ms. Lerrs appeared to be waiting for them, and she briskly hurried to the door. "Well, hello there! I am very eager to show you around. This house is so gorgeous, and I think your family will like it, but we'll see. Come into the living room first." She led them to a bright and open living room with a piano in the corner and a glass vase full of roses perched on top of the instrument

"I love how open it is in here!" Joshua said and trotted over to the piano. Mom rapidly gave Joshua a look that told him not to go any further. He received the message and swiftly came back to where he was standing originally.

"Here we have the dining room. There are doors that can close this room in, and if you have any pets, this could help. It'll also help if you desire to keep this room clean." Ms. Lerrs motioned to the next room, which was the laundry room.

Soon they went up to the bedrooms. "There are six rooms, but one is actually divided in half." Ms. Lerrs explained as they entered a huge bedroom. "This is room number one: It's the biggest one: the master bedroom. There is a pocket door that connects to a smaller room than the others. It's still pretty big, though." Ms. Lerrs led them through the pocket door into a room that was decorated with flower stickers and had pink paint on the walls.

Once they had toured the whole house, Dad and Mom told Ms. Lerrs that they would talk about this house more and would tell her their answer in a few days.

"I really loved the three acres." Grace said as she climbed into the van.

"Yeah, me too!" Melissa sat in the backseat with Leah and James, while Joshua, Grace and Isabella sat in the middle row.

"You know, there were so many bedrooms too. Was there any bad part about the house?"

"Well, the commute to work would be a bit tricky for Dad." Mom explained and Dad nodded. "And the basement wasn't finished, but that doesn't really matter! So, really, now we just have to pray, and we'll look at some other houses." The family drove along and soon came to the next house, where Ms. Lerrs met them.

The next hour was spent looking at that house, but it didn't seem to be big enough for a family of eight. There were only three bedrooms, and the backyard was only half of an acre. Shortly after touring the house, they decided to move to the next one.

"Here we are. Ooh! Look at the pool!" Melissa observed as she hopped out of the car.

"Didn't you see the pool at the first house we saw today?" Joshua asked.

"No! I must've already forgotten."

The Meadow's slowly approached the blue shuttered house. "There is a lot of land here, but all of it is far away from the house. Hmm…that's strange." James said matter-of-factly. James, lately, was trying to be more like the older children in the family- more independent and thoughtful when he spoke. Sometimes he even tried to talk like Dad in a lower voice.

"I'll be right in. If you want, grab a snack or something. I'll be there in a minute. Someone is trying to call me." Ms. Lerrs grabbed a big red bag and fumbled around until finding a burgundy phone. Ms. Lerrs wore a cozy blue sweater with a scarf and jeans.

"Okay. I think the children are getting a bit hungry anyway!" Mom picked up Isabella, who was crying. "I am going to feed Izzy. Then we'll go in. I'm assuming?" Mom asked Dad.

"Yes I can feed the kids a snack. Where would it be?"

"In the cooler. There are some apple slices and tuna sandwiches for lunch. There should be some chips as a treat too!" Mom said.

"Yum-mmy! I wove tuna!" Leah announced.

Lunch was greatly enjoyed, and Ms. Lerrs was soon off the phone. "Time to go!" Dad said.

Joshua ran out of the car and jumped up and down. "This is fun! I like to house-hunt." He suddenly slid across a muddy grass patch, landed on the pavement, and hurt his knee. "Ouch! Mom do you have a band aid?" Joshua fought back tears.

"Yes, I think I do, but give me a minute. I have to help Leah unbuckle." Mom, who looked frustrated, helped excited Leah out of the car.

"I like to house-hunt too!" Leah skipped, holding Melissa's hand.

"And here is the band-aid. It only looks like aa scrape." Mom put a brown band-aid over Joshua's scrape. Satisfied, he ran off to find James and his sisters.

"Well, I guess he's better now!" Mom chuckled to herself, and she walked next to Dad as they entered the house. The house had various paintings hung on each wall that were very interesting.

"Here is the first floor. It is very open, so you can see it all when you walk into the doorway. Let's go upstairs, now." Ms. Lerr's heels clicked on the hardwood floor. "There are four bedrooms. But they are pretty large! So, I think you could probably fit two or more in each room." Dad and Mom exchanged glances. That was one of the main reasons they were going to move: they didn't want to cram the children into rooms that they wouldn't fit.

The Meadow family made their way downstairs after touring the upstairs and all felt pretty strongly that God was not calling them to this house.

"Well, I think we are going to pray about that first house, then!" Dad announced as the family sat down to a dinner of tacos. The rest of the Meadows nodded in agreement.

Chapter Fifteen

Prayer

Now that November was here, Mom decided to start visiting co-ops like she had intended to do in October. Life was now getting extremely busy with house business, school work, and keeping up with the necessary daily accomplishments. The Meadow family was still praying about the "Hickory Valley house," as the twins called it.

"Time to go! We have to be at the "In Christ Alone" co—op in a half-hour," Mom told Grace and Melissa, who were putting the twins' shoes on.

"Okay. I have to grab my backpack... oh, and my book. I love to read on car rides! Mom, didn't you say that we have to bring our Bibles? Oh! And our notebooks?" Grace asked, briskly sprinting up the stairs.

"All right, but hurry." As frustrated as Mom felt, she tried to be joyful, and God gave her a peace.

"Mama. Weah!" Isabella pointed to Leah, who was dancing around in her dress with her backpack in her hand. "Hold! Up. Up!" Isabella softly said.

"Oh you want me to pick you up? Mommy said that I'm not big enough yet. Maybe tomorrow I'll be big enough!" One of

Leah's dirty brown pigtails sagged down to her shoulders. Just then, Grace re-entered the room.

"Mom said it's time to go. Let's get in the van. I think Joshua and James are already there. Melissa is carrying Izzy down the stairs for Mom."

"Here I am!" Melissa gracefully skipped into the room with Mom's diaper bag in one hand and a baggie full of snacks in the other. "Grace? Can you carry these? And I'll carry Isabella. Mom told us to grab bagels for the ride. Leah, can you and Grace get the bagels?"

"Yep! My arms will be full!"

"I'm sorry. I'll help you take a second trip into the house, okay?" Melissa picked up Isabella who was bundled in mittens, a coat and a cute pink hat.

"Sure!"

Soon the whole family was on their way to the co-op. "This co-op is going to have a lot of kids. I think Melissa and Grace will be together and so will Leah and James, but Joshua, I know you will quickly make a friend. All of you will." Mom focused on driving while Joshua nodded intently.

"What classes are there again?" Melissa asked as she pulled her medium- length hair into a quick braid.

"Art, Bible, gym, and choir." Mom said.

"All right we're here!" Mom parked the car. Next to them, a Mom with curly short hair got out of her own car. She unbuckled a baby, who was wearing a headband. Two kids about the ages of eight and ten walked next to her.

Mom jumped out of the car along with Grace, who was in the front seat. "My backpack!" Joshua wailed.

"Did you forget your backpack? That had your lunch in it," Mom sighed.

"Uh, yes," Joshua solemnly admitted.

"Let's try to be joyful in ALL things, even if that means you have to wait a bit for lunch. You know what? I packed an extra granola bar. That could keep you from starving." Mom handed Joshua a honey oat granola bar.

"Thanks, Mom!" They walked into a church and a lady greeted them.

"Hi, I'm Sadie Worcester. I think I talked on the phone with you. Are you visiting today?" With that, Sadie led the Meadows to the fifth- to-eighth grade class room, and Melissa and Grace walked in.

Boy! There are so many kids here! Grace thought, and she walked to a table with two girls about her age.

"I'm Lucy! Are you new here? This is my friend Lydia, and she is in sixth grade. How about you? I'm in fifth grade." Lucy talked quickly, asking Melissa and Grace questions.

"Well..." Grace began, but was interrupted by the teacher. Class was beginning!

Art class was a success, and the girls loved it! Meanwhile, Joshua had already made a friend named David. "This is the BEST gym class! This is the first time I've ever played 'flag football.' It's fun! David, what class is next?" Joshua looked at his red-haired, freckled- faced friend.

"Bible. You'll like it! It's my second favorite class." David adjusted his black framed glasses. "But...did you bring your Bible? Mrs. Smitten requires we each have a Bible."

"Oh yes, I love to read my Bible. How many kids are in this class? There must be fifty at least! What grade are you in again?" Joshua asked.

"Well, my Mom says there are twenty kids in this class-the second through fourth grade class. I'm in second grade, how about you?"

"I'm in third. I hope I get to come to this co-op every Wednesday! I love it here, and Liam, your brother is nice too," Joshua said as they entered a classroom that was painted a lush green. On the wall hung a whiteboard, which a lady was erasing. She smiled as the classmates walked into the room. She appeared to be the "Mrs. Smitten" as David described her. She had long red hair, and wore a gray sweater.

"Welcome to Bible class. Are you new to our co-op or just visiting today?"

"I'm visiting, thank you," Joshua answered as he took a seat next to David and another friend he had made.

In the meantime, Mom was enjoying a Bible study and brunch for the ladies. She was talking to a woman who said that she had five kids. She seemed to have a lot in common with Mom and they were enjoying the conversation.

"Yes, I do love homeschooling. I've been doing it for ten years now, since my oldest was in preschool. My name is Mavis by the way; Mavis Chelton."

"I'm Kendra Meadow. I have six kids. Yes, I do too! Could you tell me what comes next after this Bible study brunch?" Mom asked. Just then she noticed Sadie who was rapidly walking past her and smiled.

"Oh hi Kendra! Are you enjoying the Bible brunch?" Sadie smoothed down her frizzy short hair.

"I am, thank you!" Mom answered Sadie Worcester.

"Good! If you'll excuse me, I have to talk to my friend Bonnie who is also visiting today." With that, Sadie hurried off.

"After brunch we move into prayer groups. You can pick which one you want to attend today. My leader's name is Shelby Stevens, if you'd like to come along with me."

Soon, the co-op was over, and it was time to go home. "I woved the cow-wop! Can we go back there next week?" James asked.

"Well, I did enjoy this co-op too, but I think we should pray about it before we make any final decisions! We have two very important things to ask God about this week."

Two nights later, at the dinner table, Mom and Dad had some exciting news; they had prayed about the house and felt God's peace about putting an offer on the house, and in fact, they had just put an offer in this morning.

"Really?!" Joshua exclaimed, excited over the fact.

"Yes...and there is one more piece of news to share this evening... after praying about it, we clearly feel God's leading to go ahead and join 'In Christ Alone' Homeschool Co-op."

Chapter Sixteen

Bursting with Joyfulness

"Yay!" The children burst out in happy shouts of glee.

"We'll be starting to attend classes next week!" Mom announced. She had prepared a delicious meal of pulled pork, but the meal had been forgotten with the two pieces of exciting news. "Oh well," Mom sighed as and shook her head as she cleared the unfinished dinner off of the dinner table.

The next day was full of happiness for the children and for Mom and Dad; it was a sunny and a glorious Saturday and the Meadow family had started on a bike ride.

"Ah! It's warm for the second week of November!" Mom wore a bright yellow sweatshirt and jeans and was in a joyful mood. The night before, they had received a note from Mrs. Leither saying that she was now reading her Bible and learning more about being saved.

"You know, these past few months, I have been learning what it means to be joyful in all things. I've noticed our whole family has been choosing to be more joyful lately," Joshua noted as he pedaled through their neighborhood next to Melissa.

"Yes, I've been learning that too!" Melissa exclaimed and the rest of the family expressed that they had also been learning the gift of being joyful in all circumstances. The family pedaled along in silence, thinking about what God had been teaching them and contemplating all of the miracles God had allowed their family to witness this season.

"Wow," Melissa broke the silence and giggled. "Wow! God is amazing at how He taught our whole family this lesson together!" The family nodded their agreement.

"Yes He is!" Dad pedaled along next to Mom who had Isabella in the "bike carriage." Dad had Leah and James in his "bike carriage." Just then, stopped suddenly. Right in the middle of the side walk was a squirrel. Thinking it was a mouse, Grace gasped, but then realizing it was just a squirrel, she relaxed. Dad said, "All right, let's take a quick water break. You all seem a bit tired from what can tell." Grace nodded. She and Melissa were red from riding on such a warm, fall day. It was about sixty-five degrees!

"What time is it?" Mom asked, since she had forgotten her watch.

"It's 2:10. I think we should head back soon. What do you think?" Dad asked and took a long drink of water.

"Izzy should be getting a bit fussy and hungry soon, so yes, we should head back."

Just as the Meadow family was pulling into their driveway, Dad looked at his phone and smiled. A text read *"Your offer on the house was accepted."*

Printed in the United States
By Bookmasters